Suffolk County Council

HI-LO
K9213

D0531483

Schools Library Service

*Supporting Independent Reading
and Learning*

FULL FLIGHT

509601

Titles in the Full Flight Adventure series:

Planet Talent	David Orme
Invaders	Danny Pearson
Alien Exchange	Melanie Joyce
Camp Terror	Craig Allen
White Water	Jane A C West
Infinity Mirror	Roger Hurn
Robot Rampage	Jillian Powell
Stone End Stadium	Richard Taylor
Weed Killers	Jonny Zucker
Dynamite Deputy	Barbara Catchpole

Badger Publishing Limited
Suite G08, Stevenage,
Hertfordshire SG1 2DX
Telephone: 01438 791037   Fax: 01438 791036
www.badgerlearning.co.uk

Camp Terror ISBN 978-1-84926-583-6

Text © Craig Allen 2012
Complete work © Badger Publishing Limited 2012

Publisher: Susan Ross
Senior Editor: Danny Pearson
Series Editor: Jonny Zucker
Designer: Fiona Grant
Illustrator: Aleksandar Sotirovski

CONTENTS

CHAPTER 1	**The Journey**	PAGE 5
CHAPTER 2	**Be Warned**	PAGE 9
CHAPTER 3	**What Was That?**	PAGE 13
CHAPTER 4	**Dinner Time**	PAGE 18
CHAPTER 5	**Time to Hide**	PAGE 22
CHAPTER 6	**Time to Run**	PAGE 25

Interesting Werewolf Facts — PAGE 30

Questions — PAGE 31

New words:

midnight   terrified

prepare   marshmallows

inching   stumbling

Main characters:

Amy

Miss Johnson

Mr Wilson

CHAPTER 1

The Journey

Hi! My name is Amy Jennings.

I've always believed in zombies, vampires and werewolves, that kind of thing.

Lots of people used to make fun of me but I didn't care. I was sure they were out there; I just didn't realise I was going to come face-to-face with one.

When I heard about the trip to Scotland, I was really up for it: five days away from home; camping; midnight feasts. It sounded great.

We all met at school early on a Monday morning. The coach picked us up and we set off.

I sat by myself but that was ok; I enjoyed watching the fields go by.

After five hours we turned off the main road.

"Are you alright to get off here?" asked the coach driver.

"Not really," replied Miss Johnson, "we were told the coach would take us right up to the campsite."

The driver took a deep breath. "OK," he said, but he didn't look happy.

We'd only gone a short way when the driver pulled the coach to a sudden stop.

"I'm sorry!" he blurted out, "but I'm not going any further!"

We looked out of the window. The campsite was about half a mile ahead.

"What's going on?" asked Mr Wilson.

"You should all go home!" said the driver with terrified eyes. "Go home or you're all going to DIE!"

CHAPTER 2

Be Warned

He flung open the door and jumped off the coach.

The rest of the kids were all shouting and the teachers were trying to calm them down.

I ignored them and got off the coach.
The driver was standing under a tree.
His face was white and his hands were
shaking.

A girl called Jenny had followed me off
the coach. "Do you mind if I stick with
you?" she asked.

"Of course not," I replied.

Together, we went up to the driver.

"What did you mean about us all going to die?" I asked.

"I'm really sorry," he said, biting his nails, "but every month when the moon is full people go missing on this campsite."

"Why? Do they get lost in the dark?" asked Jenny.

"No," he replied, "they are eaten!"

Jenny burst out laughing.

I did not laugh.

"Who eats them?" I asked.

"The werewolf!" he replied, his eyes wide with fear.

CHAPTER 3

What Was That?

We had not seen Mr Wilson get off the coach. He had heard what the driver had said.

"Please do not try and scare these children with stupid horror stories!" he said angrily. "You can turn your coach back. We will walk to the campsite from here."

Everyone started getting off the coach. By now people had calmed down.

When we got to the site we put the tents up and then split into groups of four to go and collect fire wood in the forest.

I went with Jenny, and twins called Mel and Cara.

We picked up as much firewood as we could and headed back to the camp.

As we walked we suddenly heard a rustling in the bushes ahead. Jenny, Mel and Cara froze.

I picked up a stick and crept up to the bush. I counted to three in my head and then jumped around the bush to see what was there.

Standing in front of me was a giant dog
with huge razor sharp teeth.

I screamed and ran. Jenny, Mel and Cara saw the look on my face and ran after me.

"What's wrong?" asked Mr Wilson as we burst out of the forest.

"The driver was right!" I panted. "I just saw a werewolf!"

I told him about the beast I had seen.

"It was NOT a werewolf," he said crossly, "it was just a dog."

"But sir..." I said.

"No Amy!" he said. "That is enough!"

CHAPTER 4

Dinner Time

Everyone helped prepare supper.

Everyone had heard me call out to Mr Wilson about the werewolf.

There was a full moon that night and lots of people made fun out of me. But I didn't mind. I knew what I had seen.

Later on, every student sat round a big fire that we had made.

We toasted marshmallows and sung some songs.

I forgot about the coach driver and the creature I had seen. I began to relax.

This trip was going to be good.

We sat there until the fire had burned down to the last few sticks.

People had just started talking about going to bed when suddenly I noticed something strange.

"Where are Mr Wilson and Miss Johnson?" I asked.

"Maybe they went to get more fire wood," said Jenny.

But at that second we heard a horrible howl nearby.

CHAPTER 5

Time to Hide

Everyone ran.

Jenny and I dived into our tent with
Mel and Cara

They were terrified.

But I was listening.

And waiting.

There was silence for a while and then
we heard a low snort, followed by
heavy breathing.

It was not a noise a human would make.

There was silence again for a few
minutes and then we saw it...

...the shadow of a huge creature with giant teeth, inching towards our tent.

We heard a claw scrape against the side of our tent and watched in horror as the zip of the door started to slide up.

CHAPTER 6

Time to Run

The next second we heard someone yell and the sound of a struggle. There was an animal yelp of pain and then the sound of paws running away.

But then the zip of our tent opened further.

I was about to scream but a human head poked through the door.

It was the coach driver.

"I had to come back to save you all!" he shouted. "I hit it and drove it away... But it will be back! YOU ALL NEED TO GET OUT!"

We jumped out and saw his coach parked nearby. Everyone was running out of their tents and onto the coach.

"HURRY UP!" yelled the driver.

He started the engine and was about to go when I shouted, "What about Mr Wilson and Miss Johnson?"

At that second the two teachers came stumbling out of the forest. They both had cuts on their faces but they were ok.

As soon as they were on the coach the driver sped off.

We had not gone far when I looked out of the window and shouted for everyone to look too.

Against the moon was the giant shadow of a werewolf. It was leaning back on its hind legs and letting out a giant howl.

The coach sped out of the field and onto the road.

Mr Wilson and Miss Johnson went round everyone to see if they were ok.

No one made fun of me on the
way home.

Interesting Werewolf Facts

● *Werewolves are believed to be half dog and half human.*

● *Werewolves originated from myths which date back to 1591.*

● *The first report of a werewolf was in a German town called Colonge.*

● *It is thought that only silver weapons are able to stop werewolves.*

• *In Medieval Europe it was thought that if dead werewolves were not destroyed then they would come back as vampires in the form of wolves.*

• *Werewolves are believed to only appear on a full moon. When the moon is not full, the werewolves take a human form.*

• *Who knows, your school teacher may even be one!*

Questions about the Story

- *Where did the class go camping?*

- *What did the coach driver say to everyone on the coach?*

- *What did the coach driver tell Amy and Jenny?*

- *What were the names of the teachers who were on the trip?*

- *What noise scared the students so that they ran into their tents?*

- *Who was it who scared the students?*

- *What do you think happened to the teachers in the forest?*